THIS RABBIT IS
NOT FOR SALE
AND HIS NAME IS NOT
BUNNYWUNNY
IT'S STANLEY
Emily Brown

FOR
LITTLE DOG,
BOWY, BEARY
AND CAT
—FOR MANY YEARS OF
FAITHFUL SERVICE—C.C.

FOR
RUPERT,
JOHN MILK,
ELE AND THE
BIZZ — N.L.

Text copyright © 2006 by Cressida Cowell · Illustrations copyright © 2006 by Neal Layton
First published by Orchard Books in 2006   First U.S. edition, 2007
Printed in Singapore   Reinforced binding
This book is set in Filosophia Regular.   Designed by David Mackintosh
Library of Congress Cataloging-in-Publication Data on file.
ISBN-13: 978-1-4231-0645-6   ISBN-10: 1-4231-0645-8
1 3 5 7 9 10 8 6 4 2

That Rabbit Belongs to EMILY BROWN

written by Cressida Cowell

illustrated by Neal Layton

HYPERION

Books for Children

New York

Once upon a time,
there was a little girl called Emily Brown
and an old gray rabbit called Stanley.

One day, Emily Brown and Stanley were launching themselves into outer space to look for alien life-forms when there was a *rat-a-tat-tat!* at the kitchen door.

It was the Chief Footman to the Queen.
He said,

Emily Brown looked at the Queen's teddy bear.
It was stiff and new and gold and *horrible*.
It had staring eyes and no smile at all.

"No, thank you," said Emily Brown. "This rabbit is NOT for sale.
And his name isn't Bunnywunny. It's STANLEY."

And Emily Brown politely shut the door.

An hour or so later, Emily Brown and Stanley were
riding through the Sahara Desert on their motorbike
when there was a *rat-a-tat-tat!* at the garden door.

It was the Army.
The Captain saluted and said,

Her Most Royal Highness, Queen Gloriana the Third, greets Miss Emily Brown, and she would still like to have that Bunnywunny. In return, she offers her the brand-new golden teddy bear, and ten talking dolls that say "*Mama, Mama.*"

Emily Brown said, "I don't want ten talking dolls.
I want my rabbit. And his name isn't Bunnywunny.
It's STANLEY."

And Emily Brown sent that Army away, less politely this time.

A few days later, Emily Brown and Stanley were deep-sea diving off the Great Barrier Reef when there was a *rat-a-tat-tat!* at the garden door.

It was the Navy.
The Admiral saluted and said,

MAMA!

Her Most
Glorious Royalness,
Queen Gloriana the Third,
greets Miss Emily Brown,
and she would like you to
hand over that rabbit at your
earliest convenience.
She points out that she is
the poshest person on
the planet, and Bunnywunny will
be much better off with HER.
In return, she offers you the
brand-new golden teddy bear,
ten talking dolls that say
"Mama, Mama," and fifty rocking
horses that rock forever.

"I don't care WHO she is," said Emily Brown. "This rabbit belongs to ME. And his name isn't Bunnywunny. It's STANLEY."

And she sent that Navy away.

A few weeks later, Emily Brown and Stanley
were climbing through the Amazon rain forest
when there was a *rat-a-tat-tat!* at the garden door.

It was the Air Force.
The Wing Commander saluted and said,

Her Excellence, the Most Mighty Queen Gloriana the Third, greets Miss Emily Brown, and says she must have the Bunnywunny RIGHT NOW or SHE WILL NOT ANSWER FOR THE CONSEQUENCES.

In return, we will give her a brand-new golden teddy bear, ten talking dolls that say "Mama, Mama"…

Now Emily Brown was FED UP!
She sent that Air Force away, and she pinned a big notice
on the garden gate that read:

A few months later, Emily Brown and Stanley were lying fast asleep in bed, dreaming of all the adventures they would have the next day, when there was absolutely no noise at all at the door, or the gate, or the window.

Snhh!!

THE SPECIAL COMMANDOS

Silently, in crept the Queen's Special Commandos . . .

. . . and they STOLE the rabbit that belonged to Emily Brown.

When Emily Brown woke up the next morning,
for the first time in her life there was

NO STANLEY!

Emily Brown was SO CROSS.
She knew just what had happened.
She marched straight up to the Palace on the Hill.

She knocked on that naughty Queen's front door.

Rat-a-tat-tat!

Emily Brown ran into the Palace
and there was that naughty Queen, crying like
anything. The first thing she said was,

Thank goodness you've come, Emily Brown. There's something wrong with Bunnywunny!

There was indeed something wrong with Stanley.
That silly naughty Queen had put him in the royal washing machine
all night and he'd come out an odd pink color.

The Royal Dressmakers had stuffed him full of stuffing so he wasn't flippy-floppy anymore. And, worst of all, they had sewn up his mouth where Emily Brown had picked it away, and Stanley wasn't smiling anymore.

Stanley was MISERABLE.

"Oh, Emily Brown, *Emily Brown*, is there anything you can do?" asked the Queen.

"There certainly is," said Emily Brown. "**I shall take Stanley HOME.**"

The Queen started crying harder than ever. "I have all the toys in the world but none as nice as STANLEY."

Emily Brown felt sorry for that silly Queen,
so she went to the royal toy cupboard and she
took down that brand-new golden teddy bear and
she placed it on the Queen's lap.

MAMA!

Emily Brown whispered so that
no one else could hear:

*"You take that brand-new teddy bear
and you* **play with him all day.
Sleep with him at night. Hold him
very tight and be sure to have
lots of adventures.** *And then
maybe one day you will wake up
with a real toy of your OWN."*

And Emily Brown and Stanley went home.

That was the last Emily Brown and Stanley heard from
that silly naughty Queen for quite some time.

But one day, a couple of months later,
as Emily Brown and Stanley were exploring the
outermost regions of the Milky Way . . .

there came a rat-a-tat-tat! at the kitchen door . . .

It was the mailman with a letter for Emily Brown.

And it just said:

Queen Gloriana the Third

Thank you.